One hungry spider

For David and Katherine,
you made the impossible possible

Baker, Jeannie.
    One hungry spider.

    ISBN 0 86896 670 3.

    1. Numeration—Juvenile literature—
Pictorial works. I. Title.

513'.2

First published in 1982 by André Deutsch Limited. London.

This edition published in 1988 by Ashton Scholastic Pty
Limited A.C.N. 000 614 577, PO Box 579. Gosford 2250. Also
in Brisbane, Melbourne, Adelaide, Perth and Auckland, NZ.

Reprinted in 1989, 1991 and 1992.

Printed in Hong Kong.

12 11 10 9 8 7 6 5   4 5 6 7 8 / 9

One hungry spider

words and pictures by Jeannie Baker

ASHTON SCHOLASTIC

One hungry spider

spun a web between two branches.

Three birds flew close by
The spider kept still
She did not want them to see her.

Four grasshoppers came
jumping along.
One landed on the web,
but broke free
leaving a big hole.

Five dragonflies flew up
but stopped
before they touched the web.

Six spiderlings blew by on the breeze.
Three landed in the web
The hungry spider will eat them.

Seven ladybirds were flying high
One got caught but
the spider took no notice.
Spiders don't like the taste
of ladybirds.

Eight butterflies fluttered safely by.

Nine wasps hummed by.
Wasps catch spiders
so the spider left the web
and hid.

Ten noisy flies buzzed along.
Many were caught.
The spider had a feast.

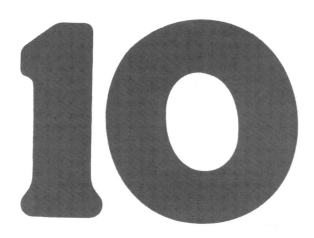

The web was torn and broken

so the spider pulled it down
and ate it.

The hungry spider is building
a new web.

The spider in this book is a female of the species called Orbweb Eriophora.

Like most web-building spiders, this one starts her web from a carefully chosen place above the ground. She squirts out a fine silk thread which is carried by the breeze through the air until the free end touches a twig, blade of grass, or other suitable support and sticks to it. The end attached to the spider's body is then fastened to a similar support and the spider crosses her 'bridge' thread spinning a stronger one as she goes. This forms the beginning of a framework from which she will then circulate to spin the rest of the web.

The spider's strongest sense is its sense of touch. They not only feel the slightest movement in the web but can identify the part of the web which has been affected. Even if an insect gets caught in the corner of the web, far from where the spider is waiting, she will find it in a flash.

If an insect lands in the web, the spider pounces at once, bites it and injects it with a poison that kills. Larger insects are first tightly bound with sticky threads, then when they can't move, bitten and poisoned.

As creatures fly or stumble into the web, they damage it. The spider will make repairs, but when the web becomes too tattered, she will recycle it by eating it before spinning a new web.

This spider is one of sixty different kinds in the Orbweb species alone. Altogether over 35,000 species of spider have been identified.